CRIC CRAC

A Collection of West Indian Stories
by Grace Hallworth

illustrated by
Avril Turner

HEINEMANN · LONDON

Distributed in the Caribbean by
Book Traders (Caribbean) Limited
Unit 33, 7-9 Norman Road, Kingston, Jamaica

William Heinemann Ltd
an imprint of Reed Consumer Books Ltd
Michelin House, 81 Fulham Road, London SW3 6RB
and Auckland, Melbourne, Singapore and Toronto
First published 1990
Reprinted 1993

ISBN 0 434 94205 7

Produced by Mandarin Offset
Printed and bound in China

Contents

Introduction

The Caribbean is a melting pot of many cultures, and two of the stories in this book, 'Rabbit and Tiger' and 'The Greedy Brother', with their South American background, show how rich and interactive these cultures are. But the majority of inhabitants in the lands that stretch from Cuba in the north to the Guyanas on the mainland of South America are of African origin and they have kept alive much of the African folklore. Therefore it's not surprising that the same tales are told – with some variations – throughout the Caribbean.

Despite the many distractions of modern life, storytelling, in the sense of oral sharing of tales, is still found in many rural areas. There may also be a significant revival, in social events which are now organised as part of a new awareness of people's 'roots' and folk traditions. Not so long ago, folk tales were also told by children at school and at play. As each child told a story he or she changed events to their own satisfaction and that story version then belonged to the child telling it.

You too can make each of these stories your own tale by telling it your own way.

Grace Hallworth
JUNE 1988

Acknowledgements

John and the Devil is my 'in memoriam' to Sotero Gomez of Lopinot, Trinidad, a most entertaining host and skilled storyteller. In his conversation he merged the 'real' and the 'unreal' so naturally that it was almost impossible to tell where the one ended and the other began.

I

The Magic Pot

When the folk character Kwaku Ananse was brought to the Caribbean, he became Brer (Brother) Anansi which is sometimes spelt Anancy or Ananci. Sometimes man, sometimes spider, he is one of the best known tricksters in folklore and there is a group of stories named after him.

This is an Anansi story which is told in many parts of the Caribbean and has a Ghanaian version called 'The Magic Plate'.

Anansi was troubled. Month after month the drought was like a monster sucking the life out of every growing thing. Soon there would be nothing left on his farm but a few stalks of corn.

One morning Anansi took a walk along a path through the forest that led to the river. There he saw a most beautiful pot with strange symbols carved on the outside. Inside it was as smooth as the stones on the riverbed.

"In all my born days I have never seen such a magnificent pot!" exclaimed Anansi. "I wonder what the symbols mean."

"Fill the pot," said the pot.

"Fill the pot!" repeated Anansi in astonishment. And before he could say more, the pot was filled with delicious chicken stew. Anansi set to at once and devoured the food.

"Ye gods and little fishes! That was a meal fit for a king. How often do you perform?" he enquired.

"As often as you like," replied the pot. "Just say the words, 'Fill the pot' and you shall have whatever you wish for. But on no account must you wash me or my magic powers will cease."

"Agreed," said Anansi at once. He had no intention of washing the pot, for he was lazy. Besides it would be easier to keep the pot a secret. He hid it underneath some bushes a little way from his house.

The very next day Anansi took the path through the forest but as soon as he was out of sight of his house, he crept into the bushes and took out the pot.

"Fill the pot!" he commanded as he wished for roasted pork and red beans.

Immediately the pot was filled to overflowing with the savoury meal. Anansi ate every morsel including the pork rind.

All that night he could not sleep for thinking of the mouth-watering food he would get from the pot. On the following day he returned to the bushes and again said the words, "Fill the pot!"

This time the pot bubbled with creamy hot *sancoche*. Yellow split peas, chunks of salted meat and a medley of vegetables floated in the thick soup. In a trice Anansi emptied the pot and licked it clean as well.

Meanwhile at home, Anansi's wife and children had to be satisfied with a daily diet of such vegetables as they found in the forest. And by the time that was shared amongst them each one received barely a spoonful. Yet every night Anansi returned home and ate his share of this meagre fare to avoid suspicion.

One day Takko, the eldest boy, said to his mother, "I think papa is up to his tricks. See how he gets fatter every day, yet he eats the same as we do."

"Child, hush yo' mouth," scolded his mother. But after that she began to watch her husband carefully. She marked the path he took and one morning she followed him stealthily and saw him eating from the pot.

"Oho!" she said to herself. "So that's his little game. Well, they say 'Every day fuh tief', but I say 'One day fuh watchman.'"

When Anansi arrived home that night his wife put his share of food before him and not a word did she say about the pot. But next morning while Anansi was still asleep, she crept out of the house and went to the place where the pot was hidden. She examined it very closely. She looked inside the pot and turned it upside down. As far as she could see it was a pot with strange signs on the outside and very dirty on the inside. So she took it down to the river and washed it thoroughly.

"Now, I'll take this to market" she said. "Perhaps someone there will know what the signs mean. In any case such a beautiful pot is sure to fetch enough money to buy some food."

Anansi was not surprised when he awoke and found that his wife had gone out. He knew that she sometimes left home early to look for root vegetables to cook: potatoes, cassava, yam, carrots, beet-root and the like. Besides, he was thinking of what he should order from the pot that day. Quickly he dressed himself and went to the hiding place – but he could not find the pot. He looked here. He looked there. He dug holes and tore up bushes. He could find the pot nowhere. Anansi thought to himself, "Maybe it went back to the river. After all it *is* a magic pot and if it can talk, what's to prevent it from walking!" He rushed down to the river. There was no pot.

Finally Anansi gave up his search and returned home.

There he found his wife with a basket of seeds for planting and a cage full of poultry. He was greatly surprised.

"Wife," said Anansi, "how did you come by all this?"

"Ah, Anansi," replied his wife, "it is a long story and a strange one. You know how I believe in my dreams. Well, last night I dreamt I saw a pot filled with food hidden not far from this house. So I got up early this morning and went to look for it. And I did find it."

"The pot, wife, the pot! What did you do with the pot?" asked Anansi impatiently.

"Well, it was so dirty that I took it down to the river and gave it a good wash before taking it to market. And just look, Anansi. I got all this in exchange for the pot."

Anansi was so angry he did not speak nor eat for many days and little by little his limbs became thin and shrivelled. But his stomach remained fat and round with all the food he had eaten. And so he is to this day.

So cric crac
Anansi break his back
For a rotten pomerac.

2

Rabbit and Tiger

The Arawaks and Warraus Indian tribes of South America tell stories about a trickster called Konehu the rabbit. He often plays tricks on Tiger.

Early one morning, Tiger was taking a walk through the forest when she heard someone making a great noise. Tiger crept forward to see who it was, and saw Konehu the rabbit pulling vines off a tree.

Tiger was surprised, for it was a strange thing to see Konehu working hard so early in the day.

"Ho Konehu!" called Tiger. "What are you doing up so early?"

"Tiger, you don't know that a big storm is coming and anyone who is not tied to a tree will be blown away?" enquired Konehu.

Of course Tiger was very worried when she heard this and begged Konehu to tie her tight to a tree.

But Konehu said, "Look Tiger, the storm will soon be here. I can't stop to bind you. Why not take these vines and bind yourself, as I shall do?"

Tiger knew that she would not be able to bind herself firmly enough, so she flattered Konehu with much sweet talk:

"You are small, Konehu, but you are so much cleverer than me in matters of this kind. I know that if you bind me, no matter how hard the wind blows, I shall be safe."

So Konehu bound Tiger tight, tight to a tree with the vines.

Then he went a little way, and began to pull more vines off another tree! Tiger heard, and chuckled to herself,

"How stupid Konehu is to think that he can bind himself to a tree. Why, the wind will blow him away at the first strong gust!"

But Konehu was only pretending. Soon he crept through the trees and went home.

Tiger waited all night for the storm to begin, but when the next day dawned clear and bright, Tiger remembered that Konehu was always playing tricks. She tried to loosen the vines that bound her, but they were firm and secure.

At mid-day the animals of the forest began to make their way down to the river.

First came Goat, with long sharp horns. Tiger greeted him: "Goat, please untie these vines that bind me fast, lest I die of hunger and thirst."

But Goat was afraid that Tiger was so hungry that she would eat him up, so he said,

"Tiger, I'll just go and sharpen my horns to loosen the knots." And Goat hurried away.

When some time had gone by and Goat did not return, Tiger again tried to bite through the vines to loosen them, but they were green and strong. Tiger would have lost every tooth before she loosened one knot.

Then came Mongoose with his sharp teeth. He was slily slinking past and looking for his enemy Snake.

Tiger called out to Mongoose, "Brer Mongoose, please untie these knots and set me free, lest I die of hunger and thirst."

Mongoose whispered, "I'll be back, Tiger, as soon as I have sharpened my teeth." And he slid away under the rotting leaves in the forest.

Soon it was late afternoon, and Tiger's throat was so dry that she could hardly raise her voice when Corbeau flew by. Corbeau's thick black feathers were glossy, for she had feasted well and was on her way to the river.

Tiger called, "Oh, my friend Corbeau, for pity's sake loosen my cords, or I shall die of hunger and thirst."

Tiger looked so weak and thin that Corbeau felt sorry for her. With her sharp beak, Corbeau untied the knots and loosened the vines and set Tiger free.

And that is why, to this day, Tiger never eats all that she kills but leaves something behind for Corbeau to eat.

Now Tiger was determined to kill Konehu the rabbit, so day after day she roamed the forest looking for him.

One day she spotted the rabbit high, high up on a rock gazing into the forest pool below. The yellow sun overhead, reflected in the water, looked like a golden ball.

"Konehu, Konehu, I am coming to kill you!" roared Tiger.

"Oh Tiger, you are just in time to witness a wonderful sight," said Konehu.

Tiger climbed right up to the rock where Konehu sat.

"What are you looking at?" asked Tiger.

"See that golden ball in the pool?" said Konehu. "If only we could get it out we would be richer than the King."

Tiger looked down at the golden ball. It was so bright that it lit up the water in the pool.

"Konehu," she said, "you are too small to lift such a large ball. Let me go in and bring it up for you."

Tiger intended to run off with the gold and keep it all for herself.

"Very well," said Konehu, "but when you get it, hold it fast. Don't let it slip from you or it will go deeper."

Quickly Tiger dived into the pool, but she soon came up spluttering and snorting. She had not found the gold.

Konehu called to her:

"Tiger my friend, be brave, be bold.
Go deep and deep to find the gold."

So once more Tiger dived down, down into the pool, into the cool water, and once more Tiger rose up puffing and blowing so hard that she sprayed Konehu where he sat high up on the rock.

Tiger was ready to give up the search, but Konehu shouted:

"Tiger, you must be brave and bold.
Go deeper still to find the gold."

This time Tiger dived deep, deep, so deep that she did not come up again.

Some say she was drowned. Others say she went so deep that she came out on the other side of the world in India, where she lives to this day.

But whichever story is true, Konehu is still laughing at how he made Tiger believe that the sun's reflection was a golden ball.

3
How Turtle
Got a Cracked Back

There are many stories about how turtle or tortoise got a cracked back. Stories which explain how and why things happened are called 'pourquoi' tales or myths.

Once Turtle had a shell as smooth and clear as a mirror. But pride goes before a fall and vanity was Turtle's downfall.

Turtle lived on the bank of a river where the forest birds flocked every morning. They came to preen their feathers and admire themselves in Turtle's shell. Each morning Turtle would ask, "What is the news, my friends?" And the birds would relate the good news, the bad news and a bit of gossip thrown in for good measure.

One morning they arrived bursting with excitement. They made so much noise that Turtle could not make head nor tail of what they were saying until Parrot flew in.

"Compère Turtle," said Parrot, "the Scarlet Ibis who live in the swamp are holding a fête on Saturday night and we are all invited."

"Not *all* of us, Turtle," sneered Peacock, "only creatures who can fly."

"Do you mean that even cockroach and mosquito can go?" asked Turtle.

"Yes, compère," replied Parrot. "It doesn't seem right that you should be left out."

Turtle didn't say a word but he thought, "If such no-good creatures as cockroach and mosquito are invited, then by hook or by crook I shall go too."

That night there was a big storm. The wind tore huge trees from their roots, and even the tall coconut palms were so badly bent that they lay with their branches flat on the ground. In the morning the birds drifted in looking like oily rags. Sadly they peered into Turtle's shell and tried to fluff up their wet feathers. Turtle watched them fluffing and preening in vain.

"Ah, my friends," he said, "you are lucky that you still have two days before the fête to dry out your feathers."

Now it was known that Turtle could foretell changes in the weather so Parrot asked, "Turtle, what is the forecast for Saturday?"

Turtle pulled his head into his shell. He was thinking. After a while he put his head out and said, "I feel the earth moving under my feet. If it continues, be prepared for strong winds and some rain."

Peacock, who was vain, said, "I for one won't go to the fête looking like a tramp. If only we could borrow your shell to use as a mirror, Turtle."

Then Turtle said as bold as you please, "If you want my shell you will have to take me with you."

"In that case," said Parrot, "we must teach you to fly."

Of course, Parrot was only joking but the birds were ready to try anything. So after a great deal of chitter and chatter each bird agreed to give some feathers to Turtle. And on Saturday night he flew off with them to the fête in the swamp.

When they arrived the birds found a quiet corner for Turtle and warned him to stay out of sight. At first all went well. The birds hopped back and forth to preen their feathers in Turtle's shell for it was indeed a windy night. Each time they came they brought delicious savouries and sweets for Turtle to feast on. Suddenly, he heard strains of music. His toes began to tingle and twitch as the music flowed through his body like an electric current. Turtle moved towards the sound of the music and began to waltz round and round. He danced with such grace that everyone crowded to

watch him. His friends the birds tried to catch his eye but the music cast a spell over Turtle. He could see nothing, hear nothing but the music.

As he danced feathers began to fall from him.

The guests began to whisper and the whispers grew to a hiss and then angry shouts.

"Intruder!"

"He's not one of us!"

"Who brought *him* here?"

"Tear off those feathers!"

"Peck his eyes out!"

When they saw what was happening the birds decided that it was time to get Turtle out. They pushed and pulled him off the dance floor and out into the tall grasses nearby. They were just in time, for the Scarlet Ibis with their long sharp beaks were flying down from their perches to see what was going on.

Turtle had just enough feathers left to fly away with the birds. But he wasn't a bit sorry for all the trouble he'd started. He boasted about his performance.

"Tonight I was king of the birds. I fly like a bird and I dance better than any bird," he crowed.

It was the last straw. The birds were so angry they stripped every feather off Turtle. He began to fall from the sky and as he fell he spun round and round until he fell *thwack*! on his back. His shell was so hard that it didn't break but cracked all over.

And ever since that day he stay just so.

4
How Tacooma Found Trouble

The simpleton or foolish person is a familiar figure in folk tales. In this story Anansi plays a trick on the simple Tacooma who believes that the name of something is the thing itself.

Anansi was always playing tricks on his friend Tacooma.

One day Tacooma asked Anansi, "What is this thing called Trouble?"

Anansi said, "Tacooma, you mean to tell me you live so long in this world and you never meet Trouble! Look, man, I will put you in big Trouble and take you out again."

"How will you do that?" enquired Tacooma.

"Just do whatever you see me do, Tacooma, and you will find Trouble."

At that moment Brer Lion's two cubs ran up and began to frisk and frolic around Anansi and Tacooma.

Now just a few days before, Lion had found Tacooma's son stealing his bananas and had clouted the boy and threatened more if he found him in his garden again. When Tacooma went to reproach Lion about it he laughed in Tacooma's face and said, "If you vex why yo' don' fight me?" Tacooma knew that he was no match for Lion so he crept away. But he had sworn that he would get even with Lion.

"Tacooma, this is your chance to get your own back on Lion," said Anansi. "Let us hide his cubs in our sacks. I'll put one in mine and you put the other in yours."

So Anansi took a-hold of one of the cubs and put it in his sack but what Tacooma didn't know was that Anansi's sack had a large hole. Then Tacooma took a-hold of the other cub and put it in his sack and tied the top tightly in a knot.

As soon as he had done so who should appear but Brer Lion.

"Mornin' Brer Lion," greeted Anansi. "We just see your two cubs running around and we holding them safe for you."

"Well, hand them over right now," said Lion. He didn't trust Anansi and he didn't care for Tacooma anyway.

Anansi opened the hole and the cub ran to his father.

When the cub in Tacooma's sack heard his father's voice he began to whine.

"Tacooma, what you do with the cub? Why you don' give it to Brer Lion?" asked Anansi. Lion looked closely and saw that the sack was tied up. He growled deep in his throat.

"How dare you tie up my cub in a sack?" he roared at Tacooma.

Poor Tacooma was so frightened that his hands trembled as he undid the knot. The cub jumped out and ran to his father who sniffed him all over to see if he was hurt. Then with one bound, Lion rushed at Tacooma who took off as fast as a hare.

> *"Run, Tacooma, run!*
> *Run for yo' life, Tacooma,"*

called Anansi.

Tacooma ran and he ran and he ran as fast as he could but Brer Lion was close behind. Anansi tried to keep up with them but they left him a long way behind.

Tacooma heard Lion's paws pounding behind him and he felt Lion's breath, and he knew that it was only a matter of time before Lion caught him. Anansi too, saw that the distance between Tacooma and Lion was getting smaller and smaller. He shouted,

"Run, Tacooma, run!
Make for short hole, Tacooma."

Lion heard Anansi call out and stopped.

"What is that yo' saying, Anansi?" he asked.

"I only say, 'Stop him before he reach short hole', Lion," said Anansi.

By the time Lion turned to resume the chase Tacooma was miles ahead and heading for short hole at the foot of a pawpaw tree.

Eventually Anansi arrived to find Lion pawing the ground outside the hole.

"Brer Lion," said Anansi, "you'll never get Tacooma out without a rope."

So Lion ran off to get a rope.

While he was away, Anansi went to the hole and called down.

"Brer Tacooma, how yo' doing?"

"Not so good, Anansi. You have to get me out of this, man."

"All right, Brer Tacooma, don't panic. Is I that get you into big Trouble, and is I who will get you out again. You listening to me?"

"Yes, Anansi, I listening good," replied Tacooma.

"Brer Lion gone to get a rope. Now, when *I* put the rope down the hole, I will call down, 'Short hand too short, lickle bit too short.'

32

But when *Lion* put the rope down I will say, 'Long hand too long, lickle bit too long.' Then you must grab a-hold of Lions's front paws and tie the rope tight tight round them. Leave the rest to me."

And so it was that when Anansi put the rope down the hole, he called out, "Short hand too short, lickle bit too short."

Then he pulled the rope out and said, "Brer Lion, my reach is too short. You take the rope and try."

Then Lion put the rope deep down the hole and Anansi called out, "Long hand too long, lickle bit too long."

At once Tacooma seized Lion's front paws and tied them tightly together with the rope. Lion thrashed about, but Tacooma pulled on the rope with all his might and held Lion fast. As soon as Anansi saw that Lion was caught, he came up from behind and tied Lion's back paws. Then he pulled him from the hole and tied him to a tree.

"Now, Tacooma," said Anansi when he had pulled him out of the hole, "didn't I promise to put you in big Trouble and get you out again?"

But Tacooma was off and away – and to this day, every time he hears the word, *Trouble*, he makes quite sure that he is not around to meet it.

5
The
Greedy Brother

Is there a man in the moon? Some people believe that there is and this story from Guyana in South America tells how he got there!

Long long ago when time was not, a brother and sister lived together in a little house at the end of the world.

After their parents died the brother said, "Sister, we must share everything *manus manus*, and I shall protect you."

"Very well," replied the sister. "I shall see to the farming and cooking while you do the hunting and weaving." So they divided everything equally between them and for a while they were both content.

One day the sister found a bee-hive in the stump of a dead tree. It was full of honey and there were no bees in the hive. So the girl scooped out the honey with her gourd and carried it home. When her brother returned from hunting she said to him, "We shall have a treat with our meat, for today I found a gourd of honey."

Now there was nothing the brother loved more than honey so he said, "Sister, give me my share at once so that I may take a little with me each day to eat on my bread." And she gave him half of the

honey. Then she covered her own gourd and hung it from the ceiling in her room. Every morning she measured out a small portion of honey for herself.

She was sweeping the hearth one day when a stone fell and she saw a jar of honey well-hidden behind the fireplace. It was the honey she had given to her brother – but none of it had been eaten.

That same night as they supped, she said to her brother, "Why don't you sweeten the porridge with some of your honey?"

Her brother replied, "I have eaten a good portion of honey already. Enough is as good as a feast."

Again, one night she said, "Brother, the bread is dry and hard. Will you not moisten it with some honey?"

And once more he refused, saying, "Sister, I must not glut myself with the honey for I have had enough today."

Each time his sister urged him to have a little honey with his food, he insisted that he'd taken his helping for the day. The girl didn't tell him that she had found his jar of honey. But she looked every day to see whether he had taken from it. The amount of honey was always the same. Well, the girl thought one thing, then she thought another. In the end she decided that a wicked spirit had stolen her brother's thoughts to make him forget.

One morning she found that the honey in her own gourd was much less than it had been on the previous day.

"Aiee!" exclaimed the girl. "The same spirit who steals my brother's thoughts at night now steals *my* honey. I shall set a trap for him this night."

So that night she rubbed her hands in the ashes and soot in the hearth. Then she climbed into bed and pretended to go to sleep. Not long afterwards, she heard stealthy footsteps, and someone came into her room. She saw the person reach up and take down the

gourd of honey. Immediately the girl sprang up, and managed to smear the thief's face with the ashes and soot. The thief ran away, but she caught a glimpse of his face. This was no spirit. The girl could not believe what she had seen. Could she be mistaken?

She could not sleep for thinking about it. Fingers of worry clawed at her mind. What could she do?

She awoke early next morning. She would prepare a fine meal.

It was later than usual when her brother came home that night. He entered the house quietly and would have gone straight to bed but his sister was waiting up for him.

"Come, brother," she called. "I have prepared a dish fit for a chief. Turtle baked in honey. A whole jar of honey!"

"A jar of honey!" cried her brother. "Where did you get a jar of honey?"

He rushed to the hearth where he had hidden his jar. As he did so,

the glow from the fire lit up his face. He had tried to clean the soot marks from his face during the day, but the harder he rubbed the more marked his face became. It was streaked with soot.

"Greedy wretch!" screamed the sister. "I shared everything with you as we agreed, and still you robbed me. You, my own brother!"

She drove him from the house and wherever she met him she shouted for all to hear, "See, one who would steal from his sister's share of food and hide his own." She told the story to anyone who cared to listen. Her brother was so ashamed that he moved further and further away from his sister and her neighbours.

At last he found himself a long way from the end of the world. He became the moon that we see in the sky.

And sometimes you can see the marks on his face where his sister smeared it with soot and ashes.

6

Put mi back where yo' find mi

The title is the punch line of a cautionary tale shared among the people of Trinidad and Tobago. From the original brief anecdote I have developed this story which has the moral: "Don't go looking for trouble".

A man was returning home from work one evening when he saw what seemed to be a baby lying under a silk-cotton tree. At first he thought that the child was dead, but when he looked closely he saw that it was breathing.

"Eh! eh!" he exclaimed, "but who leave this child here to die?"

He took the baby and, cradling it in his arms, set off home to his wife.

As he journeyed he thought to himself, "Wife will be so happy. She is always saying how quiet the house is now that all our children have left home. There'll be lots of laughter with a baby in the house."

He lengthened his stride in his haste to get home. But soon the child began to weigh heavily in his arms. From time to time he paused to catch his breath but at last he had to sit down on a stone to rest.

"Well, I ain't as young as I used to be when a mite like you can tire me out," he said to the child.

After a while he set out again with the child slung over his right shoulder.

He hadn't gone far when he felt such a pain in his shoulder he had to stop again.

As he shifted the child from one shoulder to the other, the man saw its eyes open for the first time.

"Lordy, Lordy! Is what kind of trouble I pick up today!" he cried in horror.

Quickly he put the child down.

Its eyes had no pupils. They were entirely white! What was he to do? It was hard to think straight with those cold eyes staring, staring.

Gradually the man recovered his wits and picked up the child. It seemed quite normal except for the eyes. He began to feel sorry for it.

"Poor little orphan," he said. "So that's why they left you to die! Well, wife and I will look after you, eyes or no eyes." All the same, he turned the child's head away from him. There was something about those eyes that made him fearful.

As he continued on his way, the child twined its arms around his neck and its legs around his waist, and, try as he might, he could not slacken the grip on him. There was something odd, too, about the hands and feet. He looked down and now saw a thick growth of hair covering the child's limbs – and the nails were long and pointed like the talons of a bird.

Surely this was no human baby! Now the creature was growing larger, becoming heavier with every step he took. Its hands and feet were like bands of steel around his body. He was gasping for breath

under the weight of this monstrous creature. It held him fast and would not let him go.

It was very late when he arrived home.

His wife had been watching for him and rushed to open the door when she saw him coming. There he stood holding a child – or what seemed to be a child – in his arms.

"Man, you take leave of your senses, to bring a strange child here at this time of night?" she scolded.

Her husband tried to speak, but he could not, for the creature was squeezing the breath from his body. His face was beginning to turn purple and his eyes were bulging. When the woman saw what was happening to her husband she tried to unwind the creature's arms from around his neck – but she could not loosen that iron grasp.

"Look mi trouble here tonight. This thing like it mean to kill mi husband," she exclaimed. Just then she heard the church bells ringing for evening mass and thought of the priest. She grabbed her husband's hand and, without a word, led him towards the church.

When the priest heard the story he came to the man with his holy book and his candles; but nothing he said or did made the slightest difference. The creature clung tightly to the man. The poor woman was at her wits' end. She cried, "Oh father, help my husband. Look how the wicked creature choking the life out of him."

"I have done all that I can. Now you and your husband must pray hard and ask to be forgiven of your sins," said the priest.

At these words the man began to weep. Tears rolled down his cheeks and splashed on the creature's body. Suddenly it spoke in an awful rasping voice,

"Don't hallow mi, don't drown mi
Just put mi back where you find mi."

Immediately the man felt a slight slackening of the creature's hold on him.

The three people wasted no time. The man staggered along the path which led back to the silk-cotton tree and his wife supported him as best she could. The priest brought up the rear, chanting prayers to assist them. The poor man had been carrying this burden for some time and his strength began to fail. He fell to the ground

and his wife again tried to wrest the creature's arms from his neck, crying all the while.

As her tears fell on the creature's body, it repeated the words,

"Don't hallow mi, don't drown mi
Just put mi back where you find mi."

And again the man felt a loosening of the pressure on his body.

Soon he was able to speak.

"Wife," he said, "see how the creature gets smaller."

Before she could reply, the priest put a finger to his lips warning them to be silent; but the relief on hearing her husband speak was too much for the woman. She began to sob loudly. Seeing his wife in such a state the husband, too, burst into tears which fell like raindrops on the creature in his arms.

This time it shrieked,

"Don't hallow mi, don't drown mi
Just put mi back where you find mi."

By this time they had arrived at the tree. When they looked at the creature, it had shrunk to the size of a small baby again. Its eyes were closed as though in sleep. The man laid it on the ground where he had found it.

7

How the Stars Came into the Sky

A story with Ashanti origins which is told throughout the Caribbean in different versions. This retelling was inspired by Louise Williams of Haverstock School, Chalk Farm.

Anansi had four sons. What strange children they were!

The first son had an enormous mouth which stretched from ear to ear.

The second son had bright eyes as large as saucers.

The third son was so round and fat, he looked like a large pin-cushion.

And the fourth son had such long legs that when he walked he looked as though he was on stilts.

When the children were born Anansi looked on them with shame and would not name them.

"Is who put goat mout' on you that these children come out so?" he asked his wife. But all she said was, "Anansi, one day, one day *congotay*." She loved her children dearly and brought them up to be upright, industrious boys who were admired by everyone. And after a time Anansi grew to love his sons.

One night Anansi found a large ball in the woods.

In the dark night it shone silver-bright so he wrapped it in his shirt and buried it deep in a hole.

"Such a treasure would buy a farm for each of my sons," he mused, "but the ball can belong to only one son. So what to do?"

When he got home he called his sons together and said, "I must take an important trip to find the answer to a puzzle and I want you all to come with me."

So they set out and after they had travelled for many days they came to a river. Anansi looked up and he looked down but there was nothing to take them across that wide, wide river.

"Boys, yo' see for yo'self how it is. We can't go forward so we have to turn back," he said.

"Pa, give me a chance. Let me see what I can do," said the first son.

Anansi agreed, and the boy bent down and drank up all the water

from the river. As soon as they had crossed to the other side he opened his mouth and let the water out again.

"Eh! eh!" said Anansi. "Boy, dat beat all cockfight! I never see such a thing in my life. From today your name will be Drink-a-river."

And so he was called from that day.

Well, they walked until they came to a village, and as it was getting dark they decided to rest there for the night.

Now it happened that the chief of the village had lost a beautiful jewel of great worth, and he was offering two bags of gold to anyone who found it.

When they heard about the reward, Anansi and his sons held a palaver.

"If we find the jewel there'll be enough gold for each of you to buy some land," said Anansi. And they went to the chief's house at once to offer their services. But the chief looked at Anansi's fine sons and saw a chance to get a labourer to work in his fields.

"Anansi," he said, "I will make a special bargain with you. If you find the jewel in seven days I will give you four bags of gold. However, one of your sons must remain here, and if you do not find the jewel in that time, he must work in my fields for three years."

Anansi didn't like this arrangement at all and wanted to leave the village at once but Drink-a-river, who had fallen in love with the chief's daughter, said, "Pa, leave me behind. I will work for the chief until you return."

So it was agreed, and Anansi and three of his sons set out to look for the jewel.

Day after day they searched but found neither hair nor hide of the jewel.

At last it was the seventh day. Anansi said to his sons, "Look, jump high or jump low, we must go back to the chief."

On their way back they came to some mountains which they had to cross. As they were climbing, the second son caught sight of a red glow.

"Pa!" he shouted, "look, I see something up there like a flambeau."

But the others could see nothing. It was too high up.

The boy began to climb the steep rock and at the very top he found a bird's nest. Inside the nest was a jewel which glowed red and gold in the bright sun.

In his excitement, he waved his arms to show the jewel to the others below – and lost his foothold. He began to slip and slither down the steep bare rock.

The third son saw the danger at once. He realized that he must try to catch his brother or he would be crushed on the large boulders

below. Quickly he took huge gusts of air into his lungs until he became so light that he floated upwards and cushioned his brother as he fell.

"*Sa çe courage mes garçons!* Truly you are brave sons!" said Anansi, hugging the two boys. "It was your sharp bright eyes that saw the jewel so I will call you Bright-eyes," he said to his second son. And to the third son he said, "With your body you saved your brother's life, so you I shall call Catch-Cushion."

And so they were called from that day.

Now, they had found the jewel but lost precious time. Already dark shadows were crowding out the sun's light. Evening was approaching and there was still a long way to go.

"Pa, we'll never get back in time to save our brother from the chief's bondage," said Catch-Cushion, who was beginning to tire.

Then the fourth son said, "Let me go ahead with the jewel. I think I can get back to the village before midnight."

It was agreed.

With a leap and a sprint the boy cleared the mountain ridge as if it were a mere garden fence.

"*Bonchez!* Good Lord!" exclaimed Anansi. "After that performance I shall call him Leap-over-mountain."

And so he was called from that day.

When Anansi and his two sons arrived in the village later that night, they were greeted by the chief.

"You are just in time to share in our celebrations. Thanks to you and your sons my precious jewel has been found — and you have gained a daughter."

"Daughter!" said Anansi in astonishment.

"Yes, daughter," replied the chief. "While you were away your son asked for my daughter's hand in marriage. I have given it

willingly. Do you agree?"

Of course Anansi agreed, for the girl was beautiful and sensible. So everyone was happy.

Several weeks later when all the celebrations were over, Anansi said to his sons, "We must return home, for I have found the answer to my puzzle."

As soon as they arrived home Anansi went to the place where he had buried the ball, and dug it up. Its radiance pierced the dark night and all around was as bright as day. Anansi's sons saw the light and ran out of the house to see where it came from.

"Look, my sons, look at this wonderful ball. Is it not more beautiful than the chief's jewel?"

"What is it, pa?" enquired Bright-eyes.

"It is because of this that I took you all on the journey. I wanted to find out which son most deserved the ball. But I found out that each of you deserves it equally. So, I shall throw it into the air and the one who catches it may keep it."

Anansi threw the ball as high as he could. It went up and up and up until it **shattered**!

Half of the ball remained intact but the other half broke into many different sizes and shapes. In time they became Stars and Planets. Then as the years passed the other half began to grow again. Eventually it formed a complete circle. We call it the Full Moon.

And so all Anansi's sons and their children and *their* children share equally in the light of the moon and the stars which shine so brightly in the sky at night.

8

John and the Devil

In the village of Lopinot, Trinidad, the oral tradition is kept alive through traditional festivals – especially at Christmas time – at which storytelling, singing and dancing take place. This legend was told me by Sotero Gomez who was one of the outstanding story-tellers of Lopinot.

In times past, when there were only masters and slaves, a plantation owner had a slave called John, who was the chief of all the slaves in the house. He was so clever that his master was heard to say more than once, "The slave ain't born that can equal John, and the man ain't alive that could better him – except me, his master."

One day the master's wife fell ill. She grew pale and listless, and with every passing day she became weaker and weaker. Her husband tried every kind of treatment, but to no avail. When he saw that his wife was dying he cried out in anguish, "By East and by West, by North and by South, I will give anything for my wife to be spared."

That very evening just as he was sitting down to dinner there was a knock at the door. He opened it and there stood a young man who said to him, "In the village I heard of your wife's illness and I believe that I can cure her. Will you let me try?"

The master looked the young man up and down. He seemed respectable enough, but his deep-set eyes had a strange glow which made the master uneasy. Although he was desperate enough to snatch at any straw, he wanted some assurance from this man about his skill.

"All the doctors in this land have not been able to cure my wife. Why do *you* think you can?" he enquired.

"I have knowledge of all the herbs and their powers. Besides, I'm a doctor of sorts myself," replied the stranger.

The master was not wholly convinced. But he thought to himself, "What is there to lose?" So he said, "Come, then. Let us see whether your deeds match your boast." And he took the stranger to the room where his wife lay in a coma.

The man felt the wife's pulse and listened to her heart beat, and he said, "Your wife needs more than herbs and medicine. She is already beyond death's door. Even so, I can save her – but there is a price to pay."

"I will pay any price you ask if only you are able to cure my wife," pleaded the master.

Then the stranger looked the master in the eye and said, "The price, my friend, is a life for a life. Are you willing to pay *that* price?"

The master looked into those glittering eyes and noted the cruel mouth. He knew for sure whom he faced. This was none other than the devil.

He paused for a second and then replied, "Yes, I will pay the price. A life for a life."

"Then give me John, your chief slave, in exchange for your wife."

The master didn't know what he would do without John, but he

56

thought to himself, "I have said what I have said and there is no turning back. Besides, John is only a slave and though he is valuable he cannot compare with my wife who is precious to me."

Having salved his conscience, he agreed, and the devil cured his wife.

Now earlier that night when the visitor sat down to dine with the master, John had noticed that the guest cast no reflection in a mirror which was facing him. He held his tongue but kept his eyes and ears open all evening; and it was just as well that he did, for he overheard all that passed between the two.

Two months passed. On the eve of All Souls, the master said to John, "I shall be entertaining guests tomorrow and I want you to go tonight after dinner to the coconut grove and bring me back one hundred water coconuts." Said John to himself, "Oh, ho! With all the labourers on the estate is I who must go and fetch coconuts at night. And if midnight catch me on the road, well, crapaud smoke mi pipe!" So he collected his wits and made his plans.

Now, there was a river which ran through the estate a little way from the storage sheds. John got some large sturdy branches which had been trimmed from a cedar tree and he made a dam across the river near the sheds. After dinner he set out for the grove, running all the way. Quickly he picked the coconuts and tied the stems together in small bundles. Then he set them afloat down the river and swam ahead to catch the nuts as they arrived at the dam. Long before midnight he had stored the nuts ready for the next day.

The master rose early the following morning. He was anxious to visit the coconut grove. As he was passing one of the sheds he heard someone working inside. He entered and, to his amazement, saw John chopping off the tops of coconuts and emptying the milk into a large vat.

"What the devil are *you* doing here?" asked the master.

"Why, master, I'm finishing the job you gave me last night," replied John.

"Did you return by the road?" enquired the master in bewilderment.

"Oh, no, master. I took a short cut and brought the nuts by water so that they would remain cool and fresh for your guests today."

The master was so vexed that he turned on his heel and not a word did he say to John all day.

Late that night the devil came to see the master.

"What is the meaning of this?" he demanded. "I waited for John on the road until after midnight and not a sign of him."

"Well he escaped us this time – but I'll make sure you get him next year," promised the master.

"See that you do – or it will be the worse for you," threatened the devil.

Another year soon went by, and once more on All Souls' night the master said to John, "I have asked our neighbours to join us for a breakfast feast tomorrow and I want you to pick two hundred ripe oranges from the orange grove down the estate. Pick them tonight so that they are ready for squeezing first thing in the morning."

"Oh ho! So is hide and seek again. Is I who must go and pick oranges at dead of night and if midnight catch me on the road, well, is crapaud smoke mi pipe." John stirred himself and got some barrels just large enough for him to curl up in and he had them hidden near the orange grove during the day. After dinner the master said, "John, I will come with you as far as the road. See to it that you return by the road."

As soon as the master was out of sight, John ran as fast as he could to the orange grove and made haste to pick the oranges and store them in the barrels. He fastened the lids firmly and rolled the barrels down the hill. He himself curled up in an empty barrel which rolled faster than all the others. So he got to the other end in time to collect the oranges and take them to the outhouse ready for peeling and squeezing the next day.

Long before the master got out of bed he heard John's voice

giving orders to the slaves of the household and he ground his teeth in frustration.

"Have you picked the oranges I requested?" he enquired later that morning.

"Oh yes, master. They have been picked and peeled and ready for your guests," replied John.

"And how did you bring the oranges back?" the master persisted.

"The oranges and I travelled by road and we did the journey so quickly that we were back here long before midnight," replied John.

Try as he might, the master could not discover how John managed to complete the task before midnight. He had given instructions that all the slaves be chained and closely guarded on All Souls' night. So how did John manage it?

The devil visited the master that night.

"Look here, I am becoming impatient of this delay and may have to take you in exchange," he said.

"Please believe me. I swear I don't know how he escaped from you, but he says he returned by road last night."

"I was there from eleven o'clock and nothing went by except some barrels," insisted the devil.

"Well I'll make sure that he is yours next year," promised the master.

"See that you do – or I shall certainly take you instead," warned the devil.

Time passed quickly and All Souls' approached. John was on his guard. He was beginning to tire of the game he was forced to play to save his life and soul. But there wasn't anything he could do but wait and watch.

When it was past noon and nothing had been said, John was surprised. Night came, and John went to his cabin. He went to bed,

but dared not sleep for he could not be sure of his safety until after midnight.

At about eleven o'clock he heard his master's voice outside his cabin calling, "John, John open up. I need your help."

John pretended to be asleep but the master continued to knock and call, so finally he opened the door and let him in.

"I've just come from the stables tending Nero. He's very ill and I have to go to the house for some blankets to wrap him in. Will you go and stay with him for me and wait until I return? You are the only one I trust with him."

John did not know what to think. He knew that his master loved the horse very much, yet he felt that something was not as it should be. Suddenly the master took off his cloak – a black cloak with a flaming red silk lining – and threw it over John.

"Take this," he said, "it's cold in the stables and it will keep you

warm." Now, John knew all his master's clothes, and he had never seen this one before.

John walked briskly towards the stables which were some distance away from the house. As soon as he got there, he led the horses out of the stables and set fire to the building. Then he stood in the shadows to see what would happen. Soon the master came running helter-skelter and rushed into the burning building to save his valuable horses. Sparks were flying everywhere and the master had thrown caution to the winds in his frantic search. A piece of burning timber fell on him and his clothes caught fire. At the sight of his master rolling on the ground in agony, John ran to assist him. He wrapped the black cloak around him to snuff out the flames and dragged him out of the building. Then he leapt on Nero and rode hell for leather down the road.

The night was pitch black and the devil was crouched at the side of the road, partly hidden by a hibiscus hedge. But John saw his eyes glowing in the dark and he spurred his horse on. As he sped past he called out in his master's voice, "Quick, sieze the critter before he escapes again. You'll find him wrapped in your cloak."

In the village the church bells were chiming twelve o'clock when the devil grabbed a figure huddled in a black cloak with a flaming red silk lining. The face was burnt and blackened by fire and smoke and the devil was in a hurry to get back to the warmth of his fireside before a new day dawned, so off he flew with the body and soul of the master.

No one knew what he thought when he got home and found the master in his clutches; but it is a fact that neither one has been seen in the village since that night.